Dear Parent:

Congratulations! Your child is taking the first steps on an exciting journey. The destination? Independent reading!

STEP INTO READING® will help your child get there. The program offers five steps to reading success. Each step includes fun stories and colorful art. There are also Step into Reading Sticker Books, Step into Reading Math Readers, Step into Reading Write-In Readers, Step into Reading Phonics Readers, and Step into Reading Phonics First Steps! Boxed Sets—a complete literacy program with something for every child.

Learning to Read, Step by Step!

Ready to Read   Preschool–Kindergarten
• big type and easy words • rhyme and rhythm • picture clues
For children who know the alphabet and are eager to begin reading.

Reading with Help   Preschool–Grade 1
• basic vocabulary • short sentences • simple stories
For children who recognize familiar words and sound out new words with help.

Reading on Your Own   Grades 1–3
• engaging characters • easy-to-follow plots • popular topics
For children who are ready to read on their own.

Reading Paragraphs   Grades 2–3
• challenging vocabulary • short paragraphs • exciting stories
For newly independent readers who read simple sentences with confidence.

Ready for Chapters   Grades 2–4
• chapters • longer paragraphs • full-color art
For children who want to take the plunge into chapter books but still like colorful pictures.

STEP INTO READING® is designed to give every child a successful reading experience. The grade levels are only guides. Children can progress through the steps at their own speed, developing confidence in their reading, no matter what their grade.

Remember, a lifetime love of reading starts with a single step!

To a Honey Bear named Grant
—M.S.

Text copyright © 2007 by Marilyn Sadler LLC.
Illustrations copyright © 2007 by Roger Bollen LLC.
All rights reserved. Published in the United States by Random House Children's Books,
a division of Random House, Inc., New York.

STEP INTO READING, RANDOM HOUSE, and the Random House colophon are registered trademarks
of Random House, Inc.

www.stepintoreading.com
www.randomhouse.com/kids

Educators and librarians, for a variety of teaching tools, visit us at
www.randomhouse.com/teachers

Library of Congress Cataloging-in-Publication Data
Sadler, Marilyn.
Honey Bunny's honey bear / by Marilyn Sadler ; illustrated by Roger Bollen. — 1st ed.
    p.   cm. — (Step into reading)
SUMMARY: Honey Bunny Funnybunny wants very much to be friends with the cute bear who
sits next to her in school, but he never seems to notice her.
ISBN 978-0-375-84326-6 (trade) — ISBN 978-0-375-94326-3 (lib. bdg.)
[1. Friendship—Fiction. 2. Eyeglasses—Fiction. 3. Rabbits—Fiction. 4. Bears—Fiction.
5. Schools—Fiction.]
I. Bollen, Roger, ill. II. Title. III. Series.
PZ7.S1239Hon   2008   [E]—dc22   2006015078

Printed in the United States of America   10 9 8 7 6 5 4 3 2 1   First Edition

STEP INTO READING® STEP 2

Honey Bunny's Honey Bear

by Marilyn Sadler
illustrated by Roger Bollen

Random House New York

Honey Bunny
Funnybunny
sat next to Eddy Bear.
He was the cutest bear
in school.

He had big round eyes.

He had the
best brown nose.

He had a crooked smile.

Eddy Bear made
Honey Bunny laugh.
One time he wore
two different shoes.

Another time he read

his book upside down.

And he was always
walking into walls!

Honey Bunny
liked Eddy Bear.
She wanted him
to like her, too.

So she wore
her best dress.

Then she gave Eddy
her nicest smile.

He did not
smile back!

She left a present
on Eddy's chair.
Eddy sat on it!

Honey Bunny tried
to help Eddy
in science class.

Her help was
not so helpful.

She threw him

a ball at recess.

The ball bounced
off Eddy's head.

Honey Bunny even
painted a heart for Eddy.
She put his name
in the middle.

Eddy Bear did not want
Honey Bunny's heart.

Honey Bunny

was very sad.

Eddy Bear

did not like her.

Honey Bunny did not eat
her dinner that night.

She went to bed early.

Honey Bunny felt better
in the morning.
Eddy Bear might
not like her.
But she could
still like him.

Honey Bunny ran

onto the playground.

She looked for Eddy.
The only bear she saw
was wearing . . .
glasses?

Eddy Bear was

wearing glasses!

For the first time . . .

his big brown eyes . . .

31

were looking
right at HER!